SUNDAY MORNING

A Story by **JUDITH VIORST**   Drawings by **HILARY KNIGHT**

ALADDIN BOOKS
Macmillan Publishing Company   *New York*
Maxwell Macmillan Canada   *Toronto*
Maxwell Macmillan International   *New York Oxford Singapore Sydney*

For Anthony and Nicholas,
and Alexander too

Aladdin Books, Macmillan Publishing Company, 866 Third Avenue, New
York, NY 10022. Maxwell Macmillan Canada, Inc., 1200 Eglinton Avenue
East, Suite 200, Don Mills, Ontario M3C 3N1. Macmillan Publishing
Company is part of the Maxwell Communication Group of Companies.
Printed in the United States of America
10 9 8 7 6 5 4 3 2 1
A hardcover edition of *Sunday Morning* is available from Atheneum,
Macmillan Publishing Company.
Library of Congress Cataloging-in-Publication Data. Viorst, Judith.
Sunday morning : a story / by Judith Viorst ; drawings by Hilary
Knight. —2nd Aladdin Books ed.   p.   cm. Summary: Two boys
create a lot of havoc while waiting for their parents to get up on Sunday
morning. ISBN 0-689-71702-4   [1. Brothers—Fiction.]   I. Knight
Hilary, ill. II. Title. [PZ7.V816Su 1993] [E]—dc20   92-2956

Last night my mother and father came home late.

I know because I woke up and told them
I wanted a kiss and I wanted a drink of water
and mother said shhhh, it's late
and gave me water and a kiss.

Nick was in his flag pajamas, sleeping.
She kissed him too.

Mother said good night and father said
tomorrow is Sunday and don't make noise
and don't come in our room.
We do not want to hear tie my shoes
or give me breakfast
or may I watch television.
We do not want to hear anything until 9:45 A.M.--
and <u>we'll</u> tell you when <u>that</u> is.

Okay I said. See you at 9:45 A.M., whenever <u>that</u> is.

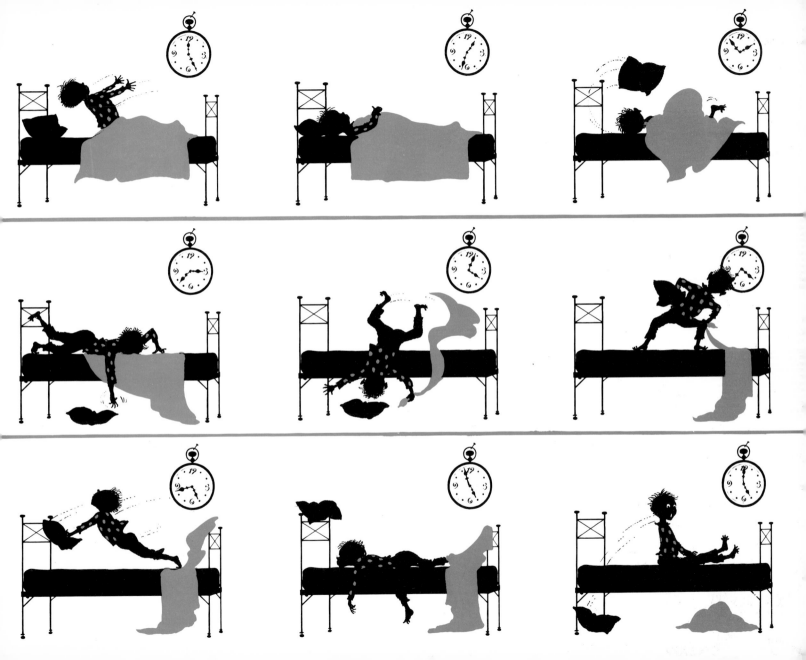

Now it is Sunday morning very early.

That Nick is still asleep.

I put on my dungarees.

I put on my socks--one blue, one brown.

(Mother says the washing machine eats socks and only leaves odd ones.)

I put on a striped shirt and black plastic boots in case there is a flood.

I wash my face and change to another striped shirt.

That Nick is still asleep.

I knock three puzzles
off the shelf.
Three puzzles are not
loud enough to wake parents
but maybe they are
loud enough to wake Nick.   No.

I make a noise like a soft fire siren.
I make a noise like a soft machine gun.

I make a noise like a soft car
crashing into a railroad train.
That Nick is still asleep.

I blow the whistle that came with my sneakers.
I blow softly in Nick's ear.

I make a gun with two fingers
and stick him in the side.
Wake up now Nick I say or else I'll shoot.
I think Nick is waking up.

Nick is awake and he is crying.

Shut up Nick I say
and take off your pajamas.
Big bully he says
and takes them off.

I get Nick dressed.
First I get
two Nick legs
into one dungaree leg.

Then I get
two Nick legs
into the other
dungaree leg.

I say he looks all right.
He says he can't walk.
I fix the dungarees.
Nick doesn't know the
zipper's in the back.

I take Nick to
the bathroom.
I wash his face.

Then we change
his shirt too.
It is still very early.
Sunday mornings are quiet.

We color.   We build a tower   Nick kicks down the tower.
We paste.   higher than my bed.   I kick Nick.

Nick writes with red crayon
on my best book.
I mash his fireman's hat.

A voice from
the other
room growls

some boys
are going
to be spanked.

Quit fighting or I'll mash <u>you</u> I tell Nick.
I trade him three beanbags for his space capsule.
We quit fighting.

I say look Nick let's get breakfast,
God I'm hungry.
He says God I'm hungry too.

We take down the dry cereal.
We take down the bowls with the animals.
We take out two spoons.
I peel the bananas.
I also pour the milk.

We get mother's dress
from the hamper
and wipe the milk.
We change our shirts again.

I put Carrots Grow
from Carrot Seeds
on the record player.
Nick says
I want to hear
Puff the Magic Dragon.

I hit him with Carrots.
He hits me with Puff.

A voice from the other room growls
some boys are going to be spanked.

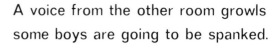

Quit fighting I tell Nick
or I'll give you a karate chop.
I trade him my cowboy belt
for his ring with the skull on it.
We quit fighting.

Nick I say let's fix the living room.
He says okay.

We take the pillows off the couch
and put them under the couch.

We put the coffee table where the blue chair belongs
and the blue chair where the other chair belongs,
and the other chair where the coffee table belongs.

The living room looks good.
Nick I say let's play a game.
The rug can be the ocean.
And you can be drowning.
When you yell help help
I will dive off the couch
and save you.
Nick says okay.
He swims around the rug for a while.

Then he yells HELP HELP.

He <u>really</u> yells help!

Mother and father come running.

Father bangs his toe on the coffee table
because that's where the blue chair was supposed to be.
Mother bumps into the blue chair
because that's where the other chair was supposed to be.

They rub their bumps and they look.
They look at Nick drowning on the rug.
They look at me diving off the couch.
They look at the living room.
They look at the clock on the mantle.
They look at each other.

And they laugh.
Good morning boys says mother.
Good Sunday morning says father.
It is exactly 9:45 A.M.

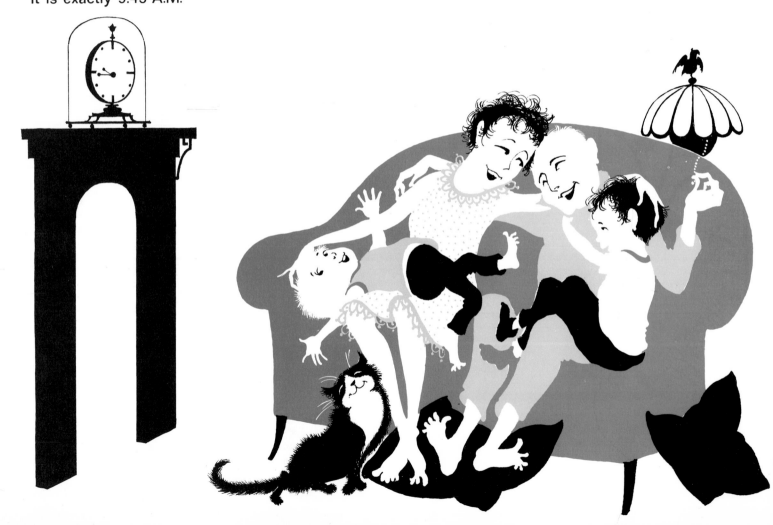